D0819727

Karg, Michael,
I am the wind /
2020.
33305251447656
ca   03/18/21

I AM THE Wind

Michael Karg

illustrated by Sophie Diao

PAGE
STREET
KIDS

Wild voices call from the cold and dusky damp.
Who says it's not a nice day outside?
I AM THE WIND!

Breathing frost and fog, I float in a barred owl's flight.
I am soft as a shadow in fields of cloud.
I pause for a moment, searching.
I AM THE WIND.

Flying northward, I find a wolverine in a flurry,
in a frolic, over snowy cornices and chutes.
I scale the highest peaks.

I AM THE WIND.

Merging with wolves, racing like a river,
the chase is on through frozen woods.
I endure for days and miles.

I AM THE WIND.

Whooshing over tundra to musk ox in massive coats,
I settle with woolly beasts on a starry polar night.
I hug my shaggy friends, hearty and warm.
I AM THE WIND.

Electrifying the heavens for a festive reindeer picnic,
I shine upon the herd as they dig and munch on moss.
I whirl and glow in shimmering waves.

I AM THE WIND.

Whistling through highlands to a snow leopard ledge,
I bound along the edge of a rocky canyon crag.
I rule this realm with gusto and grace.
I AM THE WIND.

Yodeling over Everest, I serenade some geese.
I am a mighty rush for the migratory flight.
I sing above the world.

I AM THE WIND.

Whipping up a storm for a troop of chimpanzees,
I tango under thunder in a Congo jungle show.
I holler, hoot, and howl.
I AM THE WIND.

Skimming westward on whitecaps, petrels hitch a ride.
I soar and slide with seabirds in salty foam and mist.
I sail, ever farther, ever free.

I AM THE WIND.

Climbing on a cloud to an olinguito lair,
I ease among the trees in a silvery shade.
I slip away in a whisper.
I AM THE WIND.

Bursting clumps of clouds over laughing gopher frogs,
I stir the bayou bog—a puddle-slapping spree!
I wake up the world.

I AM THE WIND.

I settle into silence
and listen for the call . . .

to lift again,

and sing   and swirl   and soar.

I AM THE WIND!

THE WIND AROUND THE WORLD

Wind stirs up the world, sending signals in scents to predator and prey, moving life-giving rain, and lifting wings of birds in flight. Whether it's a hint of a breeze or a powerful gust, wildlife know the wind and how to use it to their advantage.

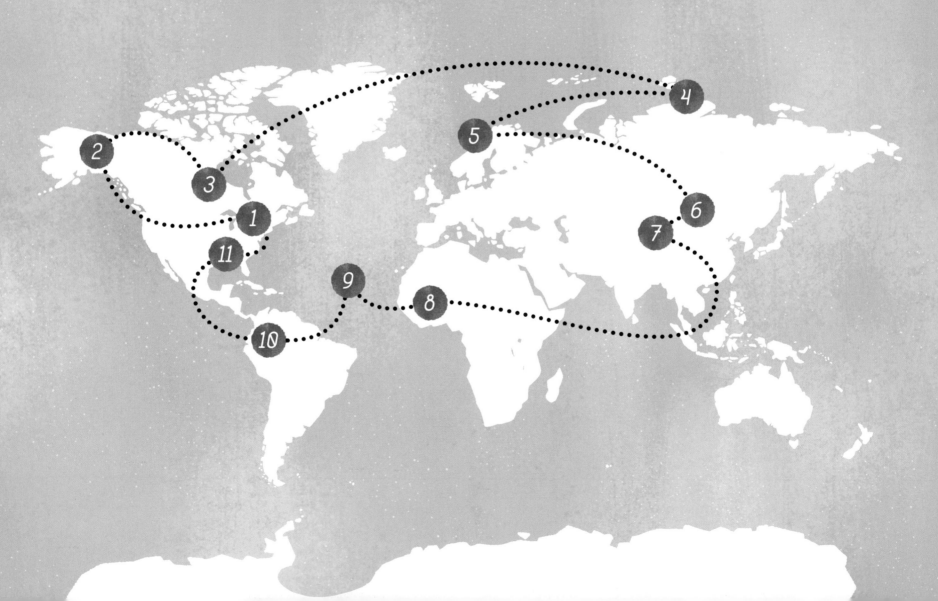

The wind met these wild creatures on our journey around the globe:

1 A **barred owl** with hungry chicks might hunt in the daytime, even though they are typically active during twilight times.

2 **Wolverines** scale snowdrifts and cliffs that even mountaineers with rope and ice tools wouldn't attempt.

3 **Gray wolves** direct elk and other large prey into deeper snow to gain an advantage in a hunt.

4 Qiviut (KI-vee-uht), the inner wool of the **musk ox**, is as soft as cashmere.

5 **Reindeer** have ultraviolet light vision which helps them find food, avoid predators, and see more color in the northern lights.

6 A **snow leopard's** long tail provides balance for making 30-foot jumps and serves as a scarf in the frigid Himalayan cliffs.

7 **Bar-headed geese** have been recorded flying above 20,000 feet as they migrate in the shadows of Mount Everest.

8 **Chimpanzees** sometimes perform ferocious rain dances in the midst of a thunderstorm.

9 **Seabirds** thrive over the open sea and can sleep while flying.

10 The **olinguito** (oh-lin-GHEE-toe) spends nearly its entire life in the trees in a cloud forest of the Andes Mountains.

11 **Gopher frogs** usually live underground but emerge to find mates after heavy rain.

BIBLIOGRAPHY

Goodall, Jane. *In the Shadow of Man*, Boston, MA, Houghton Mifflin, 1988, 52-54.

Hawkes, LA, *et al.* "The Paradox of Extreme High-Altitude Migration in Bar-Headed Geese *Anser indicus*," *Proceedings: Biological Sciences* Vol. 280, No. 1750 (7 January 2013), 1-8.

Hogg, Christopher, *et al.* "Arctic Reindeer Extend Their Visual Range into Ultraviolet," *Journal of Experimental Biology*, 2011 214:2014-2019.

Hunter, Don. *Snow Leopard: Stories from the Roof of the World*, Boulder, CO, University Press of Colorado, 2012.

Johnsgard, Paul A. *Natural Histories of North American Owls,* Smithsonian Institution Press, 2002, 190.

Markle, Sandra, *The Search for Olinguito*, Minneapolis, MN, Millbrook Press, 2017, 33.

Mech, L. David, *et al. Wolves on the Hunt: The Behavior of Wolves Hunting Wild Prey*, Chicago, IL, University of Chicago Press, 2015, 86.

Palis, John G. "Breeding Biology of the Gopher Frog, Rana capito, in Western Florida," *Journal of Herpetology* Vol. 32, No. 2 (Jun., 1998), pp. 217-223.

Rattenborg, N. C., *et al.* "Evidence that birds sleep in mid-flight," *Nature Communications* 7:12468, doi: 10.1038/ncomms12468 (2016).

Robson, Deborah, and Carol Ekarius. *The Fleece & Fiber Sourcebook*, North Adams, MA, Storey Publishing, 2011, 401.

Wolverine: Chasing the Phantom, Nature, PBS, Directed by Gianna Savoie, 13 Nov 2010.

To Chris, Ivy, Max, & Kaia.
—M. K.

For mama and baba, with love.
—S. D.

Text copyright © 2020 Michael Karg. Illustrations copyright © 2020 Sophie Diao. First published in 2020 by Page Street Kids, an imprint of Page Street Publishing Co., 27 Congress Street, Suite 105, Salem, MA 01970, www.pagestreetpublishing.com. All rights reserved. No part of this book may be reproduced or used, in any form or by any means, electronic or mechanical, without prior permission in writing from the publisher. Distributed by Macmillan, sales in Canada by The Canadian Manda Group. ISBN-13: 978-1-62414-922-1. ISBN-10: 1-62414-922-7. CIP data for this book is available from the Library of Congress. This book was typeset in Filson Pro. The illustrations were created digitally. Printed and bound in Shenzhen, Guangdong, China.

20 21 22 23 24 CCO 5 4 3 2 1

Page Street Publishing uses only materials from suppliers who are committed to responsible and sustainable forest management. Page Street Publishing protects our planet by donating to nonprofits like The Trustees, which focuses on local land conservation.

trustees

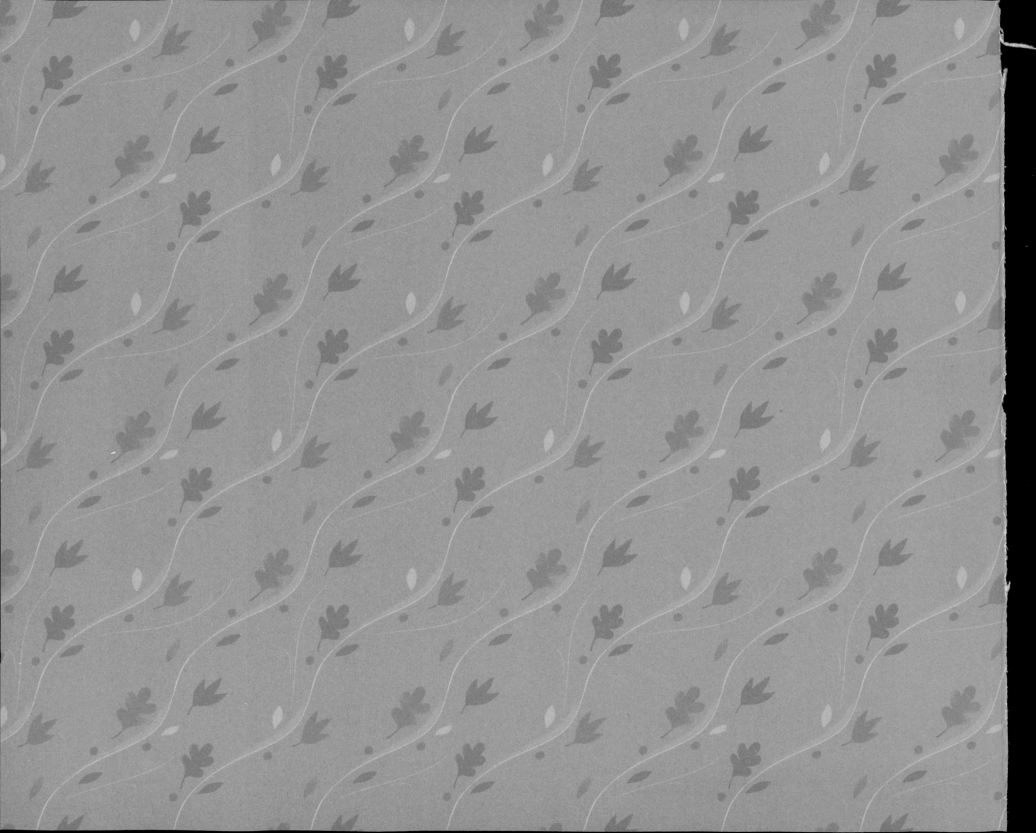